Brian the Dragon

Matt Fay

ISBN: 9798653300059

DEDICATION

To our children. Your mother and I hope this book blesses you as much as your life has blessed us.

CONTENTS

ACKNOWLEDGMENTS

Thank you to my wife, Jazzmin. She spent countless hours assisting with story writing, editing, encouraging, and listening to my ramblings as this book was written. I love you. Thank you for your never ending support.

The Ball

Brian woke up early. He stretched his small wings, twirled his skinny tail, and yawned. A single puff of smoke floated past his dull teeth and out his mouth. His adult dragon teeth had not come in yet, even though all of his friends' teeth had. Every day they made sure he remembered he was the only one that still needed knives and forks for his meals. The rest of them just used their razor sharp teeth. "I don't get to choose when my adult teeth come in," he would try to explain to them. Brian tried not to let all of that bother him though.

Once he was awake enough to flap his wings, he swooped over to his window sill where he'd left his brand new super sonic bouncy ball the night before. His heart sank when the window was wide open and the window sill was empty. He looked down from his second story window with horror. If the ball fell from this height it could be ANYWHERE!

"MOM!!!!" he yelled. "My ball is gone! Please tell me you know where it is!"

"Well, good morning to you, too! What's wrong, my little baby?" Brian's mom called back, right before she took a deep breath and blew a hot red flame from her mouth at the stone stove to cook their breakfast.

"I've already told you not to call me that," Brain mumbled. He was partly upset because he had lost his ball and partly because some of the kids at school call him a little baby, too, because of his small size. He was also upset because watching his mom blow fire so easily reminded him that he still cannot blow fire at all. "I should have blown my first fireball months ago," he thought.

"I lost my ball. Have you seen it?"

"I haven't. Sorry sweetie, but after you eat breakfast you can go look for it. Just be sure to stay in the village. Don't go past Ryu's castle. You know it's not safe to go that far alone."

Brian ate his breakfast in one bite and, to his mother's annoyance, left his plate on the table and flapped his tiny wings out the door.

Brian flew down the street in such a frenzy that he almost knocked over little Mrs. Tagamachi carrying her groceries across the street. As he flew past, he yelled to her, "Did my super sonic bouncy ball come this way?" But Brian was too worried about his ball that he flew past without giving Mrs. Tagamachi any time to answer. He faintly heard "AHHHHHH!" but he kept flying, swooping, and soaring down the hill and into the park where he saw a bunch of his classmates getting ready to play his favorite game: Castle Capture. Brian was a great seeker because he was so small and creative. He could carefully sneak into the opposing teams' castle and capture the treasure and banner. Preoccupied with his lost ball, Brian flew down to ask if they had seen it.

"Hey Bumbo! Have you seen my ball bouncing past here? Meechu? Zena? Anybody?" Brian was starting to panic.

"No, sorry Brian, but do you want to play with us?" Bumbo called after Brian.

Brian took off without even answering his best friend. The only thing he could think about was his ball. As he flapped his tiny wings, the pit in his stomach kept growing. Then, as he soared over the final hill before the jagged rocks that lead to Ryu's moat, he saw it. His ball had come to a final stop at the edge of the village. Brian was so happy! He couldn't wait to get back to the park to show his friends. Brian flew back toward the park as happy as a dragon could be, his ball clenched tightly in his claw.

"Meechu, I found my ball! Watch how high I can bounce it!" Brian happily exclaimed, not realizing he was standing right in the middle of his friends' game of Castle Capture.

"Brian, watch out!" yelled Bumbo. "We have a game going on here. We started without you because you just took off back there.

Didn't seem like you wanted to play," Bumbo's shoulders shrugged up like he was sorry.

Brian felt hurt his friends didn't want to play with him and his bouncy ball. He flew back towards his parents' castle. He was turning the last corner before getting home when he looked around and saw Mrs. Tagamachi in the same spot he saw her earlier, stooping to pick up groceries that were littering the sidewalk. It dawned on Brian that in his rush to search for his ball he must've swooped right behind Mrs. T. and scared her tail off (that's an expression that dragons use that means she was scared really badly), causing her to drop all of her groceries on the ground. Brian felt a pang of guilt. It appeared that poor Mrs. T had spent the last hour trying to pick them all up. He felt so horrible that he took the long way home so he wouldn't have to face Mrs. Tagamachi. To make matters worse, he turned around to look at all he did one last time and saw that Mrs. T. was giving the dragon boy who helped pick up her groceries a big hug and a package of Brian's favorite cookies, smokey cinnamon chip. The dragon boy was beaming at Mrs. T. as he accepted the cookies for his help. They both looked so happy.

Brian finally made it home, tired from flying so far, sad from not getting to play with his friends, and embarrassed that he had knocked an old dragon lady over. He plopped down on his favorite spot on the couch still holding his ball. Right on cue his dad plopped down next to him.

"Hey, Bri. How was your day?"

Silence.

"Do you want to talk about something that happened?" Brian's dad gently pressed.

Brian let out a sigh before starting. "I lost my ball so I went to look for it. I finally found it, but I still feel sad...and angry."

"Why do you feel that way?"

"Well, Bumbo and Meechu started playing without me at the park while I was looking for my ball, and then Mrs. T. was really upset with me because, well, I might've accidentally made her drop all of her groceries."

"Oh, I see," his dad said, "do you think you were too worried about finding your ball that you did a couple of things you're not proud of?"

"Maybe..." said Brian.

"That can happen to all of us, Bri. We dragons have a tendency to be selfish. Just remember, if you have everything you ever wanted but no one to share it with, it will feel like you have nothing at all."

"Where do you get these crazy ideas, Dad? They don't make any sense to me."

Brian's dad was silent for a little while, smiled wide and said, "Brian, I think you're ready to see for yourself." And with that, Brian's dad wrapped Brian in a big hug and walked to his office to start plans for their next adventure together.

The Great Mountain

"Rise and shine, son! We're leaving here in fifteen minutes!"

Brian couldn't believe the day of their mysterious trip had already come. He felt a flutter of nervous anticipation tickle his insides. His dad hadn't shared a single detail about the trip so Brian didn't know what to expect. All he knew was that ever since he lost his bouncy ball, his dad had been asking philosophical questions and seemed to be treating Brian tougher, or at least holding him to a higher standard. If only he hadn't lost that ball, maybe he could still be a carefree kid dragon, Brian thought to himself. The only good thing that came out of it was that Brian's best friend Bumbo was allowed to come on this 'trip' with Brian and his Dad. Probably even more excited than Brian, however, was Bumbo's mom. When Brian's dad called last week to ask if Bumbo could join, she accidentally breathed out a giant puff of smoke rings as she shrieked, "Of course he can come!" Bumbo's dad wasn't in the picture so his mom was excited for her "Bumby baby to get outside with the boys..."--and get this--she actually said "and get all smelly and dirty!"

To say a trip like this would be a stretch for Bumbo was an understatement. He didn't like the outdoors so much. Sure, he would go play ball in the park but that's about it. He never went into the woods or flew over the bay, and he surely had never stayed the night outside before. Knowing all that about his best friend, Brian was pretty confident that whatever challenge came their way this weekend, he'd be able to handle it better than Bumbo.

At 5:14 A.M. Bumbo swung his tail hard to bust open the front door to Brian's house. His mom came in behind him clearly upset about Bumbo's lack of manners, but Bumbo had a huge smile on his face, full of anticipation and excitement. Brian was happy to see his friend but did not share his same enthusiasm, it was too early for all that energy.

"Alrighty fellas! It's time to rock and roll!" Brian's dad called, bustling into the room where Brian and Bumbo stood.

"What's rock and roll, Mr. Solarux? Sounds like some kind of killer music," asked Bumbo.

"Oh, no no no, nothing that wild. It's just an old saying we used to say. Basically, when you are about to do something, you need to choose your attitude about it. Are you going to choose the rock and be stuck with a cold stone and be grumpy all day, not to mention hungry? Or will you choose the roll and be filled with nice warm bread? What will happen will happen. Your attitude is the only thing you can control."

Brian and Bumbo were still digesting what Brian's dad had just said when Brian's dad announced they were ready to go. After Brian's mom gave him a big hug and Bumbo's mom planted kisses all over Bumbo's round cheeks, Brian, his dad, and Bumbo planted their feet, bent their knees, jumped, and flew toward The Mountain. Brian and his dad had been to the mountains before, even climbed up a couple, but they had never gone to The Mountain. It was the highest peak in the range near their village. There were legends and tales of someone living at the top, but not many dragons in Edimoor village believed them anymore. Brian was pretty sure his dad still did, and that embarrassed Brian. They flew for fifteen minutes and landed at the foot of a mountain. Brian's dad looked around, took a deep breath of the pine tree scent, a dragon from Edimoor Village's favorite scent, and smiled bigger than Brian had ever seen before. Watching his dad, Brian actually thought he was starting to look younger, too. Was it just him or did his dad look taller? His back definitely seemed to stand straighter and his eyes brighter and more focused--even his wings seemed to flap with greater power. It must have something to do with the pine trees, Brian thought.

"Ok, boys, it's time to climb," Brian's dad interrupted his thoughts. "You'll have to walk most of the way. You can fly some parts of it, but not much. The trees are too dense most of the way to allow any flight, but also, you must stay close enough to the path so you know where to go. If you are tempted to leave the path or take a different route remember this: it's not worth it."

"Wait, aren't you going to be guiding us, Dad?" Brian asked, certain he must have missed a part of his dad's instructions, fear of the unknown starting to creep in.

"I'll be waiting for you every night at each camp site up the mountain, but during the day you must follow the path on your own."

Brian and Bumbo's eyes widened, and their mouths dropped open. They were partly excited for the freedom but also terrified of getting lost. Brian was speechless.

"Who made this path?" Bumbo finally asked.

Brian's dad smiled. "The same someone who created, sustains, and fights for our village and all of us. Climb the path to see. You will find out that you've always known, yet you do not truly *know* Him yet."

With that last comment, Brian's dad bent his knees, dug his clawed toes into the ground and furiously jumped, flapping his powerful wings. Brian didn't even recognize his dad at this point; he was practically glowing with might. He had never seen him so strong and powerful. Or had he always been and Brian never paid attention? He couldn't remember. Brian and Bumbo watched in awe as Dad flew away. He seemed to know exactly where to go but Brian didn't think his dad had ever been here before. Maybe Brian's grandpa took his dad once a long time ago, but that would have been thirty years ago or more. Brian's dad disappeared out of view and left Brian feeling proud that his dad was so impressive, but at the same time made Brian feel like he didn't completely know his dad. Brian and Bumbo looked at each other and knew something about this mountain was special.

Day 1: The Attack

Brian and Bumbo took their first steps along the path. It was a small and narrow dirt path through green shrubs and overgrowth. If you were looking for the path, you would know it when you saw it, but if you weren't looking for it, you wouldn't be able to certainly say one way or another if it were a path or a natural occurrence. In fact, it seemed like such an afterthought of a path that had you stumbled across it randomly, you wouldn't find any desire to follow it.

The two friends walked for over an hour before they spoke. Both, but especially Brian, needed time to process what they had just seen. They were so eager to follow the path and see what lay ahead that it was almost like they were guided along. The silence was broken when Brian and Bumbo heard rustling and breaking of branches in the forest not too far away. They froze and waited. The noise grew louder and closer. The grunting of a beast could be heard, and it was now clear that there was not one, but two beasts pushing their way through the pine trees towards Brian and Bumbo. If Brian's dad had been with them, there wouldn't have been anything to worry about. Adult dragons were big enough and strong enough to fight off any beast or creature in the woods, but Brian and Bumbo were just kid-sized dragons, and these beasts seemed hungry. With only his own safety in mind, Brian furiously flapped his small wings and flew up and away in a frenzy. Trees were whizzing by, as fast as Brian has ever flown in his life. He could still hear branches breaking from the beasts, but that was getting fainter now, actually it was silent. Curiously silent, but relief flooded. He could no longer see the path, but he didn't care. He knew he was safe from the beasts, and that was all he could think about at the moment. Far away from the danger of the beasts and the path, Brian landed on the edge of a rocky cliff, took a deep breath, and looked around. It wasn't until now that he remembered Bumbo, and Brian's thoughts began to tumble out, one after the other. Where *is* Bumbo? Why hadn't he also flown away when Brian took off? Bumbo is more than capable of flying by himself. It's not like Brian had snuck away. Bumbo could have and should have followed him. Sure, Brian left Bumbo alone with the beasts but what else was he supposed to do? And what was Brian supposed to do now that he was alone and away from the path? Would he be able to find his way back? The more Brian thought about what had happened, the more upset he became that he was now all on his own. Brian sat waiting a bit longer, long enough to calm down and start making a plan.

Brian's head began to clear. He knew he needed to find Bumbo. What would his dad say when he found out that Brian had left Bumbo to fight the beasts alone? What if Bumbo was hurt? Brian's stomach lurched. Or, what if something worse happened to Bumbo? Brian flew down off the ridge in the direction he thought he came. He flew for a couple of minutes, circled back around, and back around once more, but still saw nothing familiar. He decided to land on the ground and walk awhile because he remembered what his dad had said about not being able to see the path if you were too far away. He walked back and forth for what seemed like an hour hoping to run into the path again. At one point, he saw claw and teeth marks on the sides of the trees. He fought off a very strong urge to fly away again. In the very next moment, when Brian's fear was about to overtake him, he heard a faint yell from far off.

"Briiiiiii-aaannnnnnn," it yelled. Brian followed the sound and called back to it. He climbed for what seemed like ages and at last reached the top of a hill and saw halfway down the other side that it was Bumbo. Brian ran the last fifty feet to his friend and tackled him to the ground in a hug.

"Are you ok???" Brian asked. Brian felt so much relief seeing his best friend standing in one piece before him, but he was also a little shocked to see that Bumbo looked perfectly fine. "Why didn't you follow me?"

Bumbo's face broke into a big grin. "You're not going to believe it, but I'm actually way better than fine!"

Brian knew Bumbo had been excited about this trip, and even when they were only walking at the start of the trip, Bumbo had been enthusiastic, but now Brian saw something else. Bumbo wasn't glowing like Dad, nor was he stronger than before. As Brian stood back examining Bumbo, he could see that although his best friend was still his chubby, goofy, and clumsy self, Bumbo now stood with confidence which made him almost seem more grown up to Brian. Brian shook his head trying to make sure he was seeing Bumbo clearly.

"Well, what happened?!" Brian couldn't wait to see where this newfound confidence had come from.

Bumbo still had a big grin on his face as he started filling Brian in. "Well, I heard those beasts just like you did. I was stunned and couldn't move. When I came to my senses, I turned to look for you to see what we should do since you've been out in the wilderness before and everything, but I turned, and you were gone. I looked back at the beasts thinking I was a goner. Things started happening in slow motion, like they do when you're really scared. You know, like when that bully Thryu sneaks up on you at the park to terrorize you, or like when you..."

"Yeah, yeah, I got it, Bumbo." Brian interrupted, impatient to hear what happened next.

"Well, it was going in slow motion, like I was saying. It was too late to run, and I didn't want to leave the path because of your dad's warning, so I ducked down, planning to just cover my head with my wings. By this time the beasts were probably like ten feet away running at full speed. They launched themselves at me, jaws open and teeth chomping, trying to eat me. I was in a full-on defensive position thinking this was the end of our adventure and my life. Then, all of a sudden, my head bonked on this shield. I reached for it and picked it up. Then, almost as if it was being controlled by someone else, it spun around and attached to my claw. I didn't know what was happening, Brian. It was all so crazy!" Bumbo was almost laughing with excitement at this point in the story. "But get this, now the beasts were only a foot away. They were so close I could feel their breath on my face, but right when I squeezed my eyes shut, the shield swung at them with the most incredible force, bashing the beasts in the face and throwing them off into the distance like two hundred feet in the direction where you came from. After that happened, I was hurting so bad that I couldn't stand up for quite a while. I guess I got gashed in my back at some point," Bumbo said, turning his back to show off his battle wound. "I'm not complaining though. I would've been dead without this shield. I guess it's all about perspective, like your dad was trying to tell us earlier."

Brian was left speechless. He realized those destroyed trees he'd seen when he was trying to relocate the path must have been from Bumbo defeating the beasts. Brian couldn't wrap his head around it all. I mean, we were talking about Bumbo, the chubby dragon boy who'd befriended Brian on their first day of kindergarten by sharing his mom's homemade dragonberry scones with him. Brian wasn't sure he'd ever understand, but one thing was clear: Bumbo had been courageous, and Brian had fled like a coward. The guilt over that continued to gnaw away at Brian. He pushed it aside to congratulate his friend on his victory.

"Bumbo, that's incredible! I had no idea you were that strong!" Brian took a deep breath and pushed forward, hoping his friend would be able to forgive him. "Listen, um, I'm sorry I left you to fight off those beasts all by yourself. I feel awful knowing you were so close to…" Brian trailed off not wanting to finish the sentence. "I thought you were right behind me." Brian said, wanting to believe the words he'd just spoken. The truth was, when Brian took off, he knew that he had left Bumbo alone. Of course he'd hoped that Bumbo would follow after him…but Brian knew he was just trying to make himself feel better. Brian felt the truth burning inside him, and he heard a voice speaking the words he hadn't been able to: *he had only cared about himself.* Although it was an ugly realization that made him feel sick to his stomach, Brian finally felt better admitting the full truth, even if just to himself. Bumbo's voice interrupted Brian's thoughts.

"It's okay, Brian. I forgive you. I'm still in one piece, aren't I?" Bumbo smiled playfully.

Relief flooded over Brian. His best friend didn't hate him. In fact, he forgave him just like that. Brian had never been more grateful for a friend like Bumbo. Brian still had one last nagging question to ask. "But, what shield are you talking about, Bumbo? I've gotta see this. It sounds awesome! Maybe you can show me how to use it. Where did you learn to fight?"

"Wait, Brian. It wasn't me who fended off the beast. That's what I'm trying to tell you. I don't know how it happened, but it wasn't me. I'm *NOT* strong enough to do that, and I wasn't even prepared to fight. All I did was pick up this shield that miraculously appeared in front of me. This shield right here. I've been holding it the whole time." Bumbo held the shield out in front of him. The shield was large, made of some sort of strong and shiny metal that Bumbo could just barely see through. It glowed light blue with purple stones evenly spaced along the outer edges.

Brian scrunched his eyes trying hard to see the shield Bumbo claimed to be holding. "I don't see it, Bumbo. Are you feeling ok? Did you maybe hit your head during the attack?" Brian knew his friend had survived the beasts' attack, but he wasn't sure how. He wanted to believe Bumbo, but it seemed too unrealistic.

"I'm holding it right here, and I'm keeping it, too", Bumbo said, a little confused by Brian's inability to see the shield he was clearly holding, but he wasn't shaken. Bumbo knew what had happened back there, and it was real regardless if Brian believed him or not. He swung the shield over his back with the leather strap that had either just appeared or he hadn't noticed before.

Brian shrugged and happened to glance down. They were standing on the path! It seemed too good to be true! Immediately, he forgot all about the confusion of trying to figure out what really happened to Bumbo. He was too relieved to think about any of that. He realized that even from a few feet away, he could not see the path on his own. Earlier in his search for Bumbo and the path, he may have even walked back and forth across it a few times without noticing. He didn't quite know, but he did know three things were certain: that Bumbo survived the beasts' attack, Bumbo stayed on the path like his dad had urged, and Brian would not have been able to find the path without help from his friend. He knew he had a lot more to figure out before this adventure was over. They started walking again, and before long they looked up and saw that the sun was starting to set. They felt the warmth from the sun fade into a chill from the darkening sky. The sky was clear tonight and stars were twinkling. They stopped to sit on a rotting log on the side of the path to gaze at the stars and rest from their adventure filled day. A few minutes later, they noticed a thin ribbon of smoke drifting toward the sky about a half mile up the mountain. They suddenly remembered that Brian's dad would be waiting for them at a campsite. They stood up and half ran, half hobbled the remaining way to the fire. Brian's dad's face broke into a giant smile from horn to horn when he saw the boys approaching.

"Great job, son! Way to go, Bumbo!" Brian's dad exclaimed as he wrapped them both up in a big dragon hug, lifting their feet off the ground. "You made it through your first day, both still intact! I knew you guys would do great out there! Grab a seat and some crackers and jerky. How was it??"

The boys' faces fell at the mention of crackers and jerky. They had been climbing a rugged mountain path and encountered beasts that wanted to devour them in one gulp, all without eating, and now that they finally arrived at their campsite, all Brian's dad had for them to eat was measly crackers and jerky. Neither one of them had said this out loud, but they were half expecting a feast fit for a king after all they'd been up against. Nevertheless, they were hungrier than they remembered ever being, and so they greedily grabbed for the food and told Dad everything. Bumbo was very animated and excited when he got to the point in the story about the beasts. All the while, Brian got more nervous because he knew he would have to tell his dad where he was when this was happening. Brian noticed that his dad didn't seem surprised that Bumbo had found a shield to defend himself with. It was almost as if his dad expected Bumbo to find it. *How is finding an invisible shield that no one else can see and that has some deep hidden power inside of it not shocking?* Brian thought to himself.

Brian's dad's eyes gleamed as he spoke to Bumbo. "Incredible. I'm so proud of you for standing your ground. Your mother would have been worried sick had she been here, but you did the right thing"

"Thanks, Mr. S…I guess…I mean, I was telling Brian, and I just told you, too, that I didn't actually do any of that. I just found the shield, and IT protected me. I don't know how it happened, but if it were up to me I would've been dead."

Mr. Solarux nodded in agreement. "You're right, Bumbo. You would've been, but it was not up to you, and that is exactly why you are not dead. You chose to stay on the path. You chose to pick up the shield and have access to its protection. If you had not chosen to pick it up, you would have died. If you would've left the path, you wouldn't have found the shield. You were not the hero in saving yourself, but you played a part in it. Not to mention, you are honest and humble enough not to take credit for it all. I think for that exact reason you were allowed to keep the shield."

"Then why am I still alive since I left the path?" Brian interrupted. He so wished he hadn't flown away in his moment of panic.

Brian's dad smiled reassuringly. "Brian, you're alive because Bumbo took on both of the beasts."

Brian felt that sink in. His friend had nearly been killed fighting off those beasts, and in the end, Bumbo risking his own safety meant that Brian lived, too.

Brian's dad continued. "You boys need to have each other's backs on this trip." As he said this, he saw Brian's shoulders slump a bit. "Brian, you can do this. You have what it takes. I can see it in you right now." Brian's dad stared hard into his son's eyes, seeing his young, uncertain self staring back at him.

As the fire started to dwindle, Brian grabbed a couple more logs from close by and put them on the glowing embers. He laid his head back thinking about what his dad had just said. Earlier on the path, there were two beasts and two dragons...was one there for Brian to fight? If that was the case, was it his fault then that Bumbo got that nasty gash on his back? He supposed that made logical sense. Then it also made sense that because Bumbo did his part and more, he was rewarded. Brian still hadn't caught a glimpse of that shield all day. He so badly wanted to have a shield like the one Bumbo described. There was so much going through Brian's mind. He told himself that the next time something like this happened on the path, he would not let fear take over again. He drifted off to sleep with newfound admiration for Bumbo.

Day 2: Temptation

Brian woke to loud chewing, teeth ripping, and food tearing. It was a frightening way to wake up. He looked to where his dad had been sleeping, but he wasn't there. His dad was gone. His heart was pounding. Then behind him the ground rumbled with an enormous *THUD*, then more tearing and snapping. It sounded like something from one of his nightmares--maybe he was still dreaming. And then….BURP! "Good morning, pal!" Bumbo said with a smile. "I needed to get an early start on catching our breakfast. I didn't think I liked fish at all, but these winged mountain salmon are delicious. Maybe because I'm so hungry." Brian breathed a sigh of relief. It had been Bumbo the whole time. Bumbo was munching loudly on his breakfast and plopped down next to Brian. As the boys ate their fill of fresh fish and crackers left over from the night before, the sun was peeking over the pine trees, and there was a sharp chill in the air. When they couldn't eat another bite, they sat in silent anticipation of the day. Part of them was eager to get started and see what they would find on the path, but part of them was also worried about dangers of the unknown. When they knew they couldn't sit any longer, and they had already wasted enough time guessing and talking about the day, they stood up and took their first steps of their second day on the path.

The first few hours of the hike flew by as they took in all the new scenery that surrounded them. There were so many new types of birds, trees, and berries to see. They couldn't help themselves and tasted every berry they came across. They liked each one more than the last. Crystal clear streams and bubbling brooks appeared at different bends in the path, and after a while, the boys noticed that the same types of fish they have in Edimoor Village were here in the mountain waters, too, however, up here there was an abundance of fish whose scales gleamed and shone like gems when the sun hit them just right. In the village, overfishing had wiped out a lot of the fish populations, and the fish that remained were small and pale in color. There was something else the boys discovered about the mountain waters that they missed the first few times they had passed by--something quite unusual. The water was crystal clear, like it is in Edimoor Village, just a little colder--a welcome discovery with all the walking the boys were doing. The difference, Brian realized, was that the water was running up the mountain, instead of down. Add that to the list of things that didn't seem to make sense up here on The Mountain.

After Brian and Bumbo had gorged themselves on berries, and the excitement of their new discoveries had worn off, the hike suddenly became tiresome and repetitive. If they didn't know any better, they would have thought they were walking in circles. Brian needed to take frequent breaks because his short legs couldn't keep up with Bumbo, and Bumbo needed to take just as many breaks because his feet were killing him, and he couldn't catch his breath. Their tails kept swaying side to side off the path and either bumping into jagged rocks or getting stuck with thorns. "You know what I could really go for right now, Brian? I'd love to find a meadow and just lay down in the soft grass and sleep for hours," Bumbo said, longing for some comfort after six long, hard hours of walking. As they continued to walk along the path with their aching feet and sore backs just as far as they thought they could go, they saw a ridge fifty yards away. This, they believed, would be the change they needed. They speedily walked to the ridge to peer over and see what they could find. "Maybe up here I'll find an awesome shield like you, or maybe a sword!" Brian said to Bumbo. After seeing his dad knowingly listen to Bumbo's story about finding the shield, and now seeing all the other mysteries of The Mountain with his own eyes, Brian believed the shield was real.

They peered over the ridge, holding their breath as they looked. Their hearts sank. It was more of the same path and terrain as far as they could see. The path sloped down for a mile and then sloped back up at least another mile. They couldn't believe this day. Both boys began complaining out loud. Brian was losing hope about this big adventure and wondered what the point of such a boring and uneventful walk was. Bumbo was wondering why he had even come. He could be back in his castle with his mom eating condor eggs (a dragon delicacy), and jam on his comfortable couch. The only thing that got them walking again was realizing that they had to keep walking to make it to camp before sundown. The longer they sat at the top of the ridge, the longer it would be until they reached camp.

The downhill walk was easy, but that changed as soon as they walked one hundred yards on the up-slope. Their negative thoughts returned. Just as Bumbo released a loud, exasperated sigh, his foot came down landing on something that felt much different. He looked down to see a wide path of smooth, soft dirt. As he stood on it, he realized his feet didn't hurt anymore. This path was smooth, five times as wide as the path Brian's dad had instructed them to stay on, did not climb uphill, and looked very inviting. Bumbo's heart skipped a beat with excitement. This had to be the answer they'd been looking for! "Can you believe it?!" he practically yelled to Brian who was standing right behind him. "Brian, look, we can take this path! It looks much easier and safer. I think it'll be a lot easier to keep track of this path in the dark, too. Who knows where we'd end up following the other path. I mean, we can barely see in the daylight!" Bumbo continued on excitedly, "Oh, look, Brian! I think I see some smoke from a campfire! I bet your dad's there now. Surely he wouldn't make us climb back up all these switchbacks."

"I don't know, Bumbo," Brian said as his dad's words echoed in his head: *If you are tempted to leave the path or take a different route, it is not worth it.* "Bumbo, remember what happened the last time I left the path? I don't want to do that again."

Bumbo thought it over and remembered Brian's dad's words too, but the urge was too strong. "We have to Brian. There is no way I can make it up that hill. Plus, now I can even see a pond and a cave to sleep in. How can we pass that up? Let's just go down there to rest, and if we decide it's not the right direction then we can turn back. But we *have* to rest; *I* have got to rest." Bumbo's voice trailed off, speaking more to himself than Brian, trying to will himself to that oasis with the desperation in his voice.

Brian considered Bumbo's plan. He really would love to swim. He also was starting to think his dad was nearby this whole time so his dad would come out and make camp with them if he wasn't already down there by the pond. "I guess we can go for a little while. I'm sure we'll have to come right back, but I could use a rest too. We'll just follow the path right back to this spot after we rest. No doubt we will see it and be able to find—" Brian froze. He remembered he couldn't find the path the last time he left, and if he and Bumbo both left the path there would be no one around to help lead them back to it. Brian lunged for Bumbo's tail and yanked him back. "If we step off this path there is no telling if we will ever be able to find it again. We are going up that hill," Brian said, his voice growing more confident with each word. "You can do this, Bumbo. Have you already forgotten about yesterday? You stayed on the path instead of fleeing like me; you stood your ground against those beasts, and you rescued me. We can't walk away from that for a quick rest. You are strong and courageous, Bumbo. The path has already protected you this far."

Brian and Bumbo locked eyes, and together, moved to step back onto the narrow, winding path. They straightened their shoulders and wings and pressed on up the steep incline. With each step, they were climbing higher and higher. They began passing through the mist that circled the mountain, and he could see farther and farther as they gained elevation. Brian knew it didn't make sense, but each step seemed easier than the last. It felt like he was walking on flat ground. The hill had seemed much steeper than it actually was. Just as he was realizing this, they saw the familiar smoke rising from just off the path ahead. A sigh of relief and ten minutes of walking and laughing later, they arrived at the campsite overlooking a river. Brian's dad was waiting to envelop them in a big hug like he always did.

"Where did you get those, son?" Mr. Solarux was grinning ear to ear.

"Get what?" Brian asked, alarmed. His dad was pointing down toward Brian's feet. Brian followed his dad's pointing finger to see boots that were now on his feet. Brian's eyes widened, and he stole a glance at Bumbo who still looked confused. Brian looked back at the boots. They were black, their original color was not black but they were black now as if they had caught fire at some point. Although they'd been scorched by fire, they were in pristine condition and looked to be of the highest quality of dragon boots one could find.

"Nooooo way." Brian said, looking down again to make sure the boots were still there.

"Congratulations, Bri!" said his father. "I've only ever heard about the Boots of the Flame before...never actually seen them. In fact, all my life I've been seeking a pair for myself. I'm very impressed, son!"

"I'm confused. What are the Boots of the Flame? And why do I have them? And how did they get on my feet?"

"They were gifted to you, just as Bumbo's shield was gifted to him. They say the boots help carry you on difficult paths, and they are only entrusted to those who know the path and will not depart from it. This version, the one that is scorched with fire is a more rare edition. The flame is from helping someone escape the fire of peril that they were headed towards"

"But why me, Dad? I was the one who left the path just yesterday!"

"Brian, you learn your most important lessons from your mistakes and you stood firm today on the path. The Giver found you worthy to wear them, and all His gifts are good. We dragons tend to look at everything another dragon does wrong, but He looks at the heart."

For another time on this trip, Brian had to sift through the wise things his dad had shared with him. Brian had already learned so much about himself, and also the kind of dragon he wanted to be. As the three dragons sat quietly around the dwindling fire, the sun finished sinking down past the rocky landscape. Bumbo and Brian took one last look at the terrain that lay ahead: rocks and cliffs. The last remaining light dimmed, and the boys fell asleep as they had the night before with the fire crackling.

DAY 3: THE WALL

At first light Brian sat up and noticed his dad was already gone. How does he get up so early and sneak off so quietly, Brian wondered. Wasn't this supposed to be a father-son trip? Brian didn't know what could get his dad out of bed at such an early hour and where he could be going. Nonetheless, the boys packed up their camp like the morning before, ate some berries and nuts for breakfast, and took their first steps.

It wasn't long before the boys reached their first challenge of the day. The dirt path they'd learned to trust led them right up against a wall of boulders. This can't be right, Brian thought to himself as he scanned the rest of their surroundings to see if there was another way to get past those massive boulders. Brian and Bumbo stared at each other in consternation, neither one of them knowing what to do next. There was absolutely no way around the boulders. To the right was a steep cliff, and to the left was a smooth rock wall that looked like it went up for one hundred feet or more. The boys tossed a rock down the cliff to see how long it would take to hit another surface. They swallowed after hearing the rock hit more than ten counts later. They could have tried to fly over the boulders but they had learned their lesson about leaving the path by now. Still, they were so stumped that they were tempted to fly up just briefly to make sure the path started up again on the other side of the boulders, but that just seemed too risky after almost getting lured off the path yesterday for a rest. They didn't want to take any chances.

As they came up close to the boulders, they started to see some grooves in the rock they could climb. Brian led the way in his new boots and easily placed his foot in the first groove on the lowest rock. As soon as he did that, he noticed another foot hole for his left foot. He stretched out his foot for that hole and was already on top of the first boulder. He made a small jump to the next one, and as soon as he landed, almost as if someone was guiding him, he planted his foot into another secure holding. He glanced back at Bumbo who was able to follow Brian's exact path. The ease of finding foot holds continued until they reached the top of the fifth boulder, slid down the gradual back side on their bellies, and landed on the precious dirt path again. Almost without missing a beat, they continued walking, feeling proud that they managed that obstacle without much trouble since in the past couple of days they had really struggled through the challenges that had come their way.

Thirty minutes of brisk uphill walking later, they reached more rocky cliffs. They approached what looked like two walls of rock, each separated by about a twenty foot landing between them. They would have to climb the first wall, regroup on the landing to make a plan, and then climb the second wall. Brian approached the wall, relieved to see a boulder at the base of the wall.

"Look, Bumbo, this boulder will be perfect! I'll just climb up onto it, and then jump and grab the top of the wall. It won't be too bad, and if I need to, I can just flap my wings a couple times to clear the edge. I was able to climb over those last boulders so easily, I know I can clear this one. I'll go first."

Brian climbed to the top of the small boulder, bent his knees, and sprung up to start his jump. Just as he was pushing off, his foot slipped from the boulder causing him to fall down and hit his head. Brian popped back up, rubbing his head.

"Are you ok, Brian?"

"Yeah, I'm okay. I'm gonna try again."

"You've got this," Brian whispered to himself. "You are wearing Boots of the Flame."

Brian climbed back to the boulder, bent his knees and tried to push off, but his legs exerted no force. Then, after a split second he realized he was falling. The boulder had broken apart.

"Aghhh! Dumb boulder!" Brian yelled, partly frustrated with the situation and partly frustrated with his inability to overcome this challenge. "I was going to get it that time!"

"Now what are we gonna do?" Bumbo asked.

Brian stood there thinking, confused why his boots didn't help him this time as they did for the first group of boulders they'd had to scale.

Since Brian was so deep in thought, it felt like Bumbo was talking to himself, Bumbo continued, "I thought you were gonna make it, especially with those new boots!"

Brian snapped back to attention when Bumbo mentioned his new boots. "Yeah, that's the confusing part. I didn't have to do anything to climb those last boulders. The foot holds just seemed to appear, but it didn't happen this time."

"Sounds like how my shield works. If I try to use it under my own power, it's useless because I can't use a shield correctly. Did you try letting the boots show you the way like last time?"

"I mean, I didn't think I needed to. I thought that since they were gifted to me they were mine, and I just, kind of like, I dunno, got their power." Brian shrugged.

"No, no, no. That's not how it works. I've been thinking about all this since the first day I got my shield. I think it works like this: these items we've been gifted will protect and guide us, but it may not be the way we think they ought to. So, I think that the boots *can* still help us get up these walls, but it may not be the way we expect them to."

After further discussion about what to do next, Brian and Bumbo decided to see if some foot holds would appear on the side of the wall. Brian walked back and forth a few times and lifted his feet up the wall as high as he could. He even stood on his hands to get his feet higher. No matter where he pressed, nothing happened. Finally, after nearly an hour, they decided Brian would just have to climb onto Bumbo's shoulders and see how close he could get to the top of the wall.

Bumbo bent down, steadied Brian's feet on his shoulders and used his wings to support Brian from falling backwards. Brian reached up and was still six feet from the top, too far to jump since he was standing on Bumbo's shoulders. Just as he was about to tell Bumbo he was coming down, he grasped a crack in the wall that Brian was certain wasn't there before. He grabbed tight, pulled, and his foot struck a knob. He now had a hand and foot hold. He strained against gravity, pulling his body weight up, one knob appearing after another until he climbed the six remaining feet. He flopped his body onto the landing and rolled over to look down at Bumbo.

"How am I going to get up there? I can't reach those knobs! Brian, you can't think that I'm going to be able to---"

Bumbo's worries were interrupted as Brian yelled out, "Watch your head!" Brian threw over a rope that was already secured to a tree. It was laying in a perfectly coiled circle at the edge of the cliff. Bumbo scrambled up the rope with help from the foot holds and cracks Brian had used.

Bumbo heaved his body up over the top of the wall and flopped onto his back, catching his breath and staring up at the sky. In between breaths he managed to say, "I cannot... believe...that just...happened! That was...so...awesome, Brian! I...definitely...couldn't have...done that without...your help."

Brian looked over at his best friend and couldn't help but laugh. He realized in that moment there wasn't anyone else he'd want to be on this trip with than Bumbo. "I know, I can't believe it either! And I couldn't have done it without *your* help! If you wouldn't have thought to hoist me up on your shoulders, we might've been stuck down there all day."

Bumbo rolled over onto his side. "So, if there was already a rope fastened to that tree up here, why wasn't it already hanging down the rock wall? It does no good up here."

"I think you already answered that question earlier, Bumbo. I think it was to show us we couldn't have gotten here without each other. I tried on my own and couldn't make it. We need each other to get through all these challenges that keep coming our way."

By this time it was past noon. The boys were starting to get hungry and wondered what they would eat as they climbed the rest of the day. They really wanted some meat; they were getting sick of the berries, nuts, and crackers. They talked about each of their favorite meals as they walked. They described them in such vivid detail that they could almost smell the foods cooking in real life, and it left their mouths watering. After a little while, they snapped out of their trance and saw Brian's dad up in the distance bent over a fire. Both Brian and Bumbo thought they were still daydreaming as they came closer. Brian's dad was cooking slabs of meat and frying eggs on a hot stone over the fire. It was still only the afternoon so they were surprised to see him but welcomed the hot meal either way.

"Dad! Is this for real?!" Brian laughed as he said this, as if he couldn't believe what was before his eyes.

His dad's eyes gleamed as he said, "This is the real deal, boys, but listen, you're going to need it. You get to take it easy the rest of the day because you'll need the extra energy for tomorrow." He said as his face became serious.

Brian and Bumbo's smiles immediately vanished. Brian said, "That makes me nervous. This mountain has already been hard enough as it is. I was kind of hoping we'd catch a break tomorrow."

"It has been hard, boys, no doubt about that. But you've learned so much and come so far. You have to be strong and push through till the end. No stopping or turning back now." Brian's dad paused to let his words sink in. "And now a word of advice for tomorrow: remember that you are not alone, even when you feel like you are. Okay, my boys, enough about tomorrow. Tomorrow will worry about itself. Let's eat!"

They scarfed down the hot meal Mr. S had made them, and then filled up the last remaining space in their stomachs with all kinds of fruits Brian's dad had collected from the surrounding trees. These fruits didn't grow in Edimoor Village. They tasted like nothing you could imagine--smooth, sweet and naturally cold. A single drink of the juice had so much refreshment and flavor concentrated in it that you felt like your brain slowed down time to record all the new flavors and sensations. Forget the meat; these fruits tasted like heaven to the tired, hungry, and thirsty boys.

"We need to bring some of these fruits back to the village so we can eat this all the time!" Bumbo exclaimed.

"Sorry, guys, sadly we can't. The fruit spoils when it gets too far from the mountain. As soon as you come down off the mountain and enter the forest that we started in, it turns sour and slimy. Even if you try to take it down from this elevation it becomes less and less sweet the further down you go. The fruit and the juice is only able to be enjoyed in these high places. As you boys now see, there is nothing else like it, and it is always worth the hard and long journey to get up here."

The boys rested, took naps, ate, and drank more throughout the day and evening. The sun was finally setting, and it was time to get some real sleep for the night. The boys didn't want this day to end, but they both started to get the feeling that something greater was waiting for them. They both allowed sleep to take them.

Day 4: Isolation

Brian woke to Bumbo loudly smacking his lips, slurping his juice, and gnawing at some boar bacon that Brian's dad had cooked before heading out that morning. Brian scrambled up, slightly annoyed to have been woken up that way but quickly forgot his frustration when he realized that he also got to eat boar bacon and more of that divine fruit juice.

The boys only stopped eating when they physically couldn't fit any more inside their stomachs. They stood up to walk, and after a few steps, realized they had eaten way too much. They felt sluggish and tired already, but they knew they had no time to waste. They probably had already wasted too much time as it was. After thirty minutes of walking through cool, crisp air, they worked off their sluggishness and started making their normal pace. Brian's heart raced at every turn and at the top of every hill. He knew today was the day they were to reach the top of the mountain and got to see for themselves what this whole trip was about.

After thirty more minutes of walking, they came to a level clearing. The clearing was surrounded by thickets, thorns, and vines. The path entered the circular clearing and exited out the other side. Hammered into a large rock in the middle of the clearing was a wooden post about three feet high with a sign on it. The boys slowly approached. As they stepped closer to the center of the clearing, the sounds of all the animals, wind, water, and other music the mountain played faded away. It was an eerie silence. Brian read the sign aloud.

You are nearing the end of the climb, but this is just the beginning of your path. Ahead lies beauty so complete that you cannot bear to look directly at it, terrible trembling or absolute comfort, and richness beyond measure but of no value to this world.

Before you can continue, one of you must complete this task: Return to the camp by the river and retrieve a scroll from under the rock that looks like a trout and return here. The other of you must wait here until he returns; do not exit the clearing. Start right away. Finish strong.

Bumbo looked at Brian. Brian looked at Bumbo and then dropped his gaze. Brian's heart was pounding because he didn't want to be the one to have to go all the way down to the camp. His boots started to feel curiously warm, too, as if they were full of energy and asking to run. Despite Brian knowing what he should do, he'd already made up in his mind what he would do. He knew Bumbo well enough to know that if he could outlast this awkward silence, Bumbo would take the task; he always did. The seconds felt like they were stretching on into eternity, both boys silent. Brian's boots were burning hot at this point. He began shifting his weight to relieve some of the pain. He couldn't give in now. He just had to outlast Bumbo a little longer. If this was any other moment he would allow them to carry him at a break-neck pace up the mountain--but not now. Not *down* the mountain all by himself, where there were beasts, where there was no fire lit by his dad, no help for the challenges along the way, where who knows *what* could happen. Finally, Brian heard Bumbo take a breath to speak. Brian exhaled all the breath he'd been holding in. He made it. He was in the clear.

"The campsite by the river was two nights ago," Bumbo said, trailing off, more to himself than to Brian. Bumbo looked into Brian's eyes as if giving him one last chance to step up to this challenge. They both knew Brian was far more physically cut out for this challenge than Bumbo was, but still Brian said nothing. Bumbo took a deep breath as if to ready himself, then took off. Just as Bumbo was reaching the edge of the clearing Brian called after him, "You got this B. I know you'll make it."

Brian was relieved he wouldn't have to walk the whole way back, but he was stung by a sharp pang of guilt as the back of his friend disappeared over the ridge. He felt useless, like he was a spectator on his own climb. Brian looked up at the sun and guessed it had to be mid morning still. He figured Bumbo could make it down to the camp and back up by midnight tonight, figuring he would make great time going down and better time than they did coming up since he would already know the way. He also wouldn't have the couple hours of trying to figure out how to climb that wall because he would just leave the rope hanging over on his way down. Brian sat with his back against the sign post and waited; there was nothing else to do.

As if they knew their moment had passed, Brian's boots finally cooled off. He couldn't help but wonder what would've happened had he allowed his boots to carry him through this challenge. He would never know. Brian's mind continued wandering, this time in a different direction: how peaceful it was and how he had never heard quietness like this before; he quite liked it. He then thought back to the Village, how he was always running from one thing to the next--meeting friends at the park and being endlessly worried about looking cool, smart, or strong to kids he barely even knew at school. He had never found quietness like this in the city, and he wasn't looking forward to going back to the loud, busy life he lived in the Village. Out here, Brian didn't have any self-conscious worries; he could just *live*. He sighed and sank his weight into the sign post. He dug his claws into the dirt to let some fall through his fingers. A small, cool breeze blew past Brian's ears. He heard a faint whisper as if the wind or the trees had spoken to him. "Who are you, Brian?" It asked.

"Who am I?" Brian said aloud to himself. This question brought him deep into thought. He had never, ever thought about it before. Out here in the silence was the perfect place to process it, but he still didn't know. He wanted to fit in and be accepted by his friends at school, or at least make them think he was cool. Was this still important? If not, what was? He knew he was stronger now than he had been when they started (even though he ignored this last prompting to rise to the final challenge). This new strength was now part of who he was. He knew he felt most proud of himself when Bumbo had nearly strayed from the path, and Brian had grabbed his friend to pull him back to the path.

He knew these were clues, but there were still holes. Maybe some of the holes would have been filled in had he gone down the mountain like his heart--and boots--had been telling him to. He resolved right then to never miss another opportunity like that again. Somehow he knew that if he kept ignoring the feelings in his heart, and especially this one in his boots, he would stop noticing them so much. The intensity would fade; he would be sucked back into his lonely, isolated world where he only cared about his lost bouncy ball again. He kicked himself for missing this one challenge that was so obviously for him.

Brian continued thinking through his life in reverse to try to pick up more clues. He pictured his dad's strength and mystery that he had been noticing this whole trip, how his dad was stronger here on this mountain. Something clicked for Brian that he'd never thought of before, though it seemed like such common knowledge: his dad is part of who Brian is. Seeing his dad in this new light actually changed the way Brian saw some things. His respect for his dad grew knowing that he was steadfast in his beliefs and didn't waver when Brian was embarrassed or when people misunderstood him. This was now impressive to Brian because he saw his dad on this mountain and knew him more fully. His dad wasn't dorky, weird, or embarrassing.

The sun was starting to set now, and Brian was getting hungry. He stood up to walk around the clearing to see if there was anything to eat. He circled it a couple of times but saw nothing. His stomach furiously growled as he spotted some berries and nuts about ten feet into the brush, just past the clearing. He wanted them so, so badly, but he remembered the sign, and how poorly it always turned out when he tried to make his own plans. So he waited. Bumbo should be back in an hour or so anyway. One hour passed, then two. Brian soon wore a dirt path into the grass from walking back and forth from the sign post to the entry path to try to peer over the incline to see Bumbo. Brian couldn't see or hear anything.

Another hour passed, and by this time Brian could only see a few feet in front of him. He walked back in the direction of the nuts and berries. He didn't think he could resist at this point. He approached the much desired food and was reaching for a stick in hopes to be able to at least clear a path to the nuts and berries. As he reached for the stick he heard that small whisper again, "Who are you, Brian?" He froze upon hearing this question once again. Immediately, it was so clear to him that this was an opportunity to show who he truly was, the Brian that had always been inside of him, waiting to be put through the refining fires of hardship and challenge to produce character that shines like gold. In the same instant Brian felt this deep assurance rest upon him, but doubt wasn't far behind invading his thoughts. Was he making too big of a deal out of everything that had happened this weekend? Had he really heard an actual voice asking him that deep life question? Was there an actual point to this whole weekend, other than his dad trying to recreate an adventure-filled weekend he once had with his own dad? What if these nuts and berries were here to sustain him while he waited for who knows how many more hours until Bumbo returned and his challenge was actually to get them or starve? Brian shook his head, as if to scatter the confusion from his mind.

He wondered what his dad would do in this situation. He didn't need to think long; his dad wouldn't try to bend the rules. Plus, if Bumbo had to walk all those miles on his own then Brian could wait here for him. He slowly walked back to the middle of the clearing and started to get a little worried about his friend. There was nothing he could do for him though, so he laid back and closed his eyes.

He woke up to the sun peeking over the horizon. He laid there, half awake, enjoying the quiet and warmth. When his brain was awake enough to register how hungry he was, it sat him bolt upright. The next thing that registered with him was that Bumbo hadn't made it back yet. He stood up and ran toward the edge of the clearing, overcome with worry and dread for his friend. He had to go find Bumbo! What happened to him out there? Had another beast come and eaten him? Had he gotten lost or fallen off the cliff while it was dark? Why hadn't Brian just gone ahead and traveled with him--what did that dumb sign know anyway? The worry he felt for Bumbo left him feeling sick to his stomach. He was at full speed now, going to sprint past the clearing and down the path, completely forgetting, or ignoring his task to stay inside the clearing. He was one step away from exiting when he crashed into something soft.

He landed on his back and looked up. He had run right into Bumbo's big belly. Bumbo grinned a goofy and proud grin showing off the scroll and a sack full of fruits and vegetables that he must have grabbed along the way. Brian breathed an enormous sigh of relief, and for another time on this trip, he felt overwhelmed with thankfulness that his friend had returned safe and sound, and also that Brian's lack of courage to step up to the plate had not ended in ruin. The boys ate, rested, and caught each other up on what had happened while they'd been separated.

THE SUMMIT: FACE TO FACE

With the challenge being completed and behind them, they gathered their things and made their way to the exit of the clearing. They walked right by the nuts and berries Brian had been so tempted by the day before. Brian took a moment in his mind to acknowledge the small victory he'd experienced in not giving in to that temptation. Just up ahead, the red rocky terrain gave way to vibrant green grass and moss covering the mountainside. Flowers in full bloom danced in the breezy mountain air. The boys raced toward the thick, lush grass and sprawled out on it. They had never seen or felt grass so green and so soft.

They looked around and saw a few large oak trees along the path and a sparkling river flowing. It almost seemed like they had entered a new country and were no longer on the mountain. They slowly walked toward the middle of the grassy plain; they didn't choose to--they were just drawn that way, floating almost. A little ways away, resting against a large oak, were a couple of hikers they'd briefly encountered at the base of The Mountain. These hikers looked older and more experienced than Brian and Bumbo. They carried packs weighed down with every kind of tool, snack and supply you could ever need, whereas Brian and Bumbo carried nothing with them except the gifts they'd received along the way.

Since Brian and Bumbo recognized the two hikers from earlier, they approached them, excited to see other dragons again. Maybe they'd sit down together and swap harrowing stories of their adventures from the last few days. As the boys drew closer, however, they realized the other hikers were not resting at all. They were hunched over with their knees drawn to their chests, cowering and shaking with fear and dread. The boys stopped in their tracks.

"What happened to you two?" Brian asked, confusion and fear in his voice.

Without even looking up to see who had approached them, one of the dragons replied, "It's terrible! HE is terrible! Teeth…..claws….fire...we can't bear to look!"

The other dragon whimpered, "He's right up there on the jagged rocks, just past the bubbling mud pits blocking our path. We don't want to be bothered. If He would just let us be..." the dragon trailed off.

"Jagged rocks? Mud?" Bumbo mumbled, confused. He and Brian only saw the beautiful blue sky, thick grass, and crystal clear stream ahead. Words began to tumble out of Bumbo's mouth before he'd even thought about what he would say. "Didn't you make this journey to see Him?" Bumbo hadn't planned those words but he knew they came from his heart. Looking back on this whole experience, he knew something had saved them and guided them up the mountain this whole time. He couldn't help but remember Brian's dad's words from the first day about "knowing who made the path."

"Are you crazy?!" the dragon who'd spoken first replied, finally bringing his head up to look at Bumbo and Brian. "That would be suicide! We set out to conquer this mountain because everyone says it can't be conquered."

Brian felt his boots start to warm again, fainter than before, but clearly generating extra heat. He even felt a slight force from them urging them forward past the tree. "By the looks of you two, it seems to me that everyone was right. Come on, Bumbo. Let's go see Him for ourselves...see if He's as terrible as these guys are making him out to be," Brian said.

After leaving the petrified dragons cowering in fear, Brian and Bumbo walked a little while longer, crossed the water on a footbridge, and started ascending to the highest peak. Although they were climbing to the highest point of the mountain, the ground beneath their feet was still covered in soft, thick green grass. When they were almost to the top of the peak, they were knocked down to their knees by a force and brilliance of light that was indescribable. They were both on their knees before they could think. They tried to lift their heads up but it felt impossible; they didn't raise an inch. After what could have been five seconds or five hours, they heard a voice with the strength of a thousand waterfalls say, "Look up, child." Only then could they raise their heads and see what was ahead. "Come receive your crown." Although Bumbo was still there, the utter magnitude of the moment made Brian unaware of Bumbo's presence.

Brian inched forward and reached out for the crown that the giant dragon held out. This giant dragon was three or four times the size of Brian. He was a majestic purple in color, wearing a crown, eyes filled with power and determination, and had claws sharper than anything Brian had ever seen. His beauty was so great that Brian's eyes filled with tears. Brian didn't feel safe being this close to the dragon, but the only thing he could do was obey. "Ask your question," the giant dragon said.

"What…" Brian's voice quivered with both fear and awe. He cleared his throat and tried again. "What…is your name?" Brian asked.

"I am the Giver of good gifts, the Healer of all wounds, the Maker of paths, the Breath of Edimoor Village and beyond, and the Great Dragon on The Mountain." The Great Dragon said, devoid of any kind of arrogance or pride. He knew he had nothing to prove; he was just answering the question. "I am the way through this passing age. Those against me will not survive the coming breath of fire, but those with me will be refined by it and protected."

"It was you helping us this whole way, wasn't it?" Brian asked.

"It was, and it was me before you found yourself on this mountain, too. You just chose not to see me, but you have now chosen to see me. Why did you resist my love for so long, Brian?."

A cold shock went through Brian from his horns to his tail. He felt so foolish letting so many meaningless things consume his mind. With this hindsight he could see countless times that he resisted the Great Dragon's guiding claw. How plain it was now to Brian that Edimoor teemed with the Breath of the Dragon. Embarrassment turned into sadness and then into resolve in a matter of moments. "I chose my own way because I thought it would be better or more fun. I was wrong on both of those. I am sorry, I never want to choose that way again." Brian humbly stammered. "We couldn't have made it without you. Thank you for your help, Great Dragon, sir, erm...however you would like to be called, your Highness?" Brain squeaked.

The Great Dragon's laughter caught Brian off guard. It rumbled loud and deep like thunder. "You are a great joy, Brian. I'm glad you recognized your dependence and weakness, though. That is the point of climbing The Mountain," the Great Dragon said. A slight smile creeping across his face.

Brian wouldn't have been able to explain it in the moment, his senses were too overwhelmed with all the sights and feelings he was experiencing, but as soon as he asked forgiveness of the Great Dragon he knew nothing more of those sour feelings. They had been cast away and he truly believed it when the Great Dragon called him a great joy. At that moment he felt absolutely pure. That if there was a calm pool of water to look at his reflection he would not have seen a skinny little dragon cub, but a strong, tall dragon plated with shiny gold with no blemishes. This must be how the Great Dragon always saw him, it would surely explain how he could pursue Brian without ceasing even with all the mistakes and messes he had made. "What is this crown?" Brian asked, nearly bursting with excitement. The embarrassment and fear so far from his mind he was able to speak freely and joyfully.

"It is the Crown of Life. A seal of ownership from me to you. Others that don't have the crown will not be able to see it, but that doesn't make it any less powerful. You completed the climb. You are strong and courageous. You stood firm on the path like a solid oak. You freely gave yourself to help your friend up the climb, and you humbled yourself and accepted help along the way. The ones who try to elevate themselves are overwhelmed with dread when there is nothing to dread. Fear nothing because you have my seal. This is just the beginning, Brian. You must now go back to the Village and live these things out. You must show others the Way and point them to the Mountain Path."

When He finished speaking, the Great Dragon was gone, but the feeling of his presence lingered. Bumbo was standing next to Brian again wearing a crown, just as Brian was. They were speechless, but there was also nothing to say. They both knew what the other was thinking, and they knew their friendship had just grown into a brotherhood.

They sat on the slope for a while in silence, but there was no awkwardness. In fact, somehow the silence brought them closer. After some time, Brian's dad flew in and landed next to the boys. Brian's dad's eyes glistened with tears, and he was beaming horn to horn, like Brian had never seen before. "I'm so proud of you boys. I knew you would make it."

Brian's eyes widened as he looked at his dad. "Have you had that your whole life?" Brian asked, just now noticing his dad's crown.

Brian's dad's eyes twinkled. "Not my whole life. Your grandpa set me off on an adventure like this when I was about your age. But that's a story for another time. Come on, boys, let's go home."

ABOUT THE AUTHOR

Matt lives with his wife and son in Indianapolis, Indiana. He works in the healthcare field and writes for pleasure and for the purpose to inspire a love of books, wonder, mystery, and excitement in his kids. This book is his first attempt.